DANNY ORLIS
AND THE
BIG INDIAN

&

DANNY ORLIS
SECOND STRING FORWARD

DANNY ORLIS AND THE BIG INDIAN

&

DANNY ORLIS SECOND STRING FORWARD

BERNARD PALMER

Danny Orlis and the Big Indian, and Danny Orlis Second String Forward
© 2023 by Bernard Palmer
All rights reserved. First edition 1956.
Second edition 2023.

Scripture quotations from The Authorized (King James) Version. Rights in the Authorized Version in the United Kingdom are vested in the Crown. Reproduced by permission of the Crown's patentee, Cambridge University Press.

Cover image: Adobe Firefly
Character illustrations: John Ball
Editor: Charlene Miskimen

Aneko Press Youth

www.anekopress.com

Aneko Press, Life Sentence Publishing, and our logos are trademarks of Life Sentence Publishing, Inc.
203 E. Birch Street
P.O. Box 652
Abbotsford, WI 54405

JUVENILE FICTION / Religious / Christian / Action & Adventure

Paperback ISBN: 978-1-62245-964-3

eBook ISBN: 978-1-62245-965-0

10 9 8 7 6 5 4 3 2

Available where books are sold

CONTENTS

HIDING THE PLANE

The sun is always slow to get out of bed in December in northern Minnesota, and Danny Orlis, Bob, and Tex had had breakfast and were out at the airport warming up the engine of Tex's light plane before the first faint gray streaks of dawn came poking up over the horizon.

Danny stood there impatiently while Tex let the motor idle. There were low, heavy clouds hanging along the skyline, the sort of clouds that could be carrying a blizzard in their teeth.

Danny bit his lower lip. He just had to get home. He couldn't be weathered in here at Bemidji.

Tex was noticing the clouds, too. Danny saw him studying them out of the corner of his eye. And only a moment or two ago he had stopped at the airport office to learn the latest weather report.

Tex was one of those cautious pilots who had logged thousands of hours over the bush country without a fatal accident. If the storm got bad, he would either set down where they were or turn and run from it. Or if the weather report sounded ominous, he was likely to insist that they stay in Bemidji until after the storm. And at that time of year it could mean days of waiting.

"Come on, guys," Tex said now, moving to loosen the ropes that anchored the ski plane to the ground. "Let's get our stuff aboard and get on our way. Everything's all right now, but we've got a bit of bad weather boiling in out of the West."

"I thought it was cold in Colorado," Bob shivered as he loaded his bag into the plane, "but I never saw it this cold before."

"It is a little frosty, all right," Tex laughed. "Twenty-two below. But the heater in this new plane's a lot better than the one in the Stinson."

"This is a new plane, isn't it?" Danny echoed as they started to move down the runway. "How come?"

"We piled up the old one," the pilot answered shortly. "That's how your dad got hurt."

Danny looked at him quickly. It was the first time he could remember that anyone had ever been hurt flying with Tex. His dad always said that he felt safer up in the air with him than he did sitting in the living room at home. What was it the flier had said when Danny had asked him about the accident the day before?

"I wish I knew how it happened," he had answered. "And why."

Danny looked over at Bob. There were questions in his cousin's eyes.

Tex nosed the sturdy little plane upward until they reached an altitude of 1500 feet. Then he headed straight north to Baudette and angled across the frozen, snow-covered Lake of the Woods toward Angle Inlet and Danny's home.

The big lake stretched below them, white and motionless in the grip of the biting cold. Bob looked down and shuddered, but Danny smiled expectantly.

"Hey, isn't that beautiful?" he asked, more of himself than his companions.

"I guess maybe you could call it that," Bob replied nervously. "But I'll be mighty glad when we get on the ground again."

The clouds had come stealing across the sky to blot out the sun, and now and then snow went streaking across the windshields. The little plane bucked stubbornly in the wind.

Tex turned on his deicers and checked the compass again, glancing quickly at his passengers as he did so.

"Getting sick?" he asked. Danny shook his head, but Bob could only grin weakly.

"There's some snow in this," the pilot told them, "and it's moving in faster than the weather report said."

Bob gulped hard.

"Do–do you think we'll make it?" he asked.

Tex checked his compass again, although he was flying over territory he had been over a thousand times. The clouds below them were beginning to close in until they could only catch fleeting glimpses of the ground.

Danny leaned forward and peered down. In a little rift in the clouds he could see Oak Island, lying silent and white beneath them, and he could just make out American Point and Magnuson's Island ahead. Although he hadn't noticed, the pilot had been gradually losing altitude until now they were flying in swirling snow at about 350 feet.

"The ice on the creek is smooth," Tex said as he banked expertly and went gliding down. "We'll land there and taxi up close to the house."

Danny's mom came running out to meet them, her parka hastily thrown over her dress. She hugged Danny, and in spite of herself cried a little.

"You and your mom had better go on into the house, Danny," Tex said. "Bob will stay out here and help me get the plane up to the house and tied down before the storm gets too bad."

Danny looked strangely at the pilot. Tex had been flying to Angle Inlet for years and had never before insisted on bringing his plane right up next to the house to stake it down for the night.

In the cabin Danny found his dad sitting up in bed, his big Bible on his lap.

"I certainly hated to have Mom call you out of school this way, Danny," he said. "But I can't deny that I'm very glad to have you home."

"I'm very glad to be here," Danny answered. "How are you feeling, Dad?"

Mr. Carl Orlis grinned at him crookedly. "If I felt any better," he said, "I'd be out running my trapline."

Danny wanted to ask his dad a thousand questions. He wanted to find out about the accident, how it came to happen with an experienced pilot like Tex, why Tex was acting so strangely, and why he insisted on bringing his plane up next to the house. But Bob and the pilot came in just then, stomping the snow off their feet.

"It's getting mighty cold, Carl," Tex's big voice boomed from the kitchen. "I think we're in for a real storm."

"Sounds like it," the injured man agreed. "Do you think you've got the plane in a safe place?"

Tex had come into the room by this time. Danny looked from him to his dad and back again.

"I brought it right up next to the house and covered it with canvas," the pilot said. "After it snows for an hour or so, no one'll know it's there."

"Unless they heard you come in," Mr. Orlis cautioned. "Then they'll know that the plane's got to be around here some place, and they'll hunt until they find it."

Tex nodded, his mouth drawing down to a thin, hard line. "Don't worry," he said softly. "I'm going to keep my eyes open."

"What's wrong?" Danny asked them. "Why do you have to hide the plane? What's happened here, anyway?"

"That's a long story, Danny," Mr. Orlis said gravely. "We'll tell you all about it some time."

Something about his tone warned Danny not to ask questions. Instead, he and Bob sat there, staring at one another, their minds racing.

CHAPTER 2

WHO FOUND THE PLANE?

Mrs. Orlis came in before long and called them to dinner.

"You and the boys can eat in the kitchen," Mr. Orlis said. "But I'd like to have Tex bring his plate in here where he can talk to me. We've got some matters to go over."

"Now, Carl," Mrs. Orlis started to protest, "let him eat at the table with–" She stopped suddenly. "All right," she said. "I'll get you a tray, Tex."

Danny saw all of that, but said nothing.

"I'm so glad that you boys are here, Danny," his mom said after she had taken trays in to Tex and her husband and Danny had asked the blessing. "You don't know how uneasy I felt being here in the house alone with Dad hurt so badly that he hasn't even been able to get out of bed."

"What–" Bob started to ask, but Danny kicked him sharply on the shin and shook his head.

It continued to snow all afternoon—a fine, drifting snow that piled high over the plane and was heaped against the buildings in huge white hills. Tex didn't make any effort to leave. He had been weathered in at Angle Inlet before. The only thing to do was to sit and wait until the storm blew itself out.

Danny and Bob helped Mrs. Orlis with the dishes and brought in wood for the stove and heater.

"This beats going to school, doesn't it?" Danny grinned.

"You can say that again." There was a long silence. "What do you suppose they're going to do with[1] Eric?" he asked.

"I'm afraid it won't be easy for him," Danny said. "They've got a lot of evidence against him."

"I know," Bob went on. "But it doesn't seem fair somehow. He got his car wrecked and is going to spend a month or so in the hospital. That certainly ought to be punishment enough without sending him to the detention center too."

"The law has its own punishment," Danny answered. "It's just like it is in the Bible. Some people seem to think that they'll be punished here on earth for the things they do. And, I guess a lot of people are punished that way, just like Eric was with his accident," he continued. "But the Bible tells us that the wages of sin is death. And,

---

[1]   Eric Tanner, who took a bribe from gamblers to lose a high school football game in *Danny Orlis Makes the Team*.

if we haven't trusted Jesus as our Savior, we're going to have to pay the penalty, just like Eric. And it won't make much difference whether we've suffered here on earth or not, as far as God's punishment is concerned."

Bob sat for a long while staring out the window at the driving snow.

"I probably haven't lived a perfect life," he said defensively, "but I don't think I've been so bad."

"The Bible tells us that we're all wicked," Danny countered. "It says that none of us have been seeking after God and living the way we know we should. So, if we're all sinners, and the wages of sin is death, then we all are lost unless we've accepted Christ as our Savior."

Bob got to his feet angrily.

"You ought to preach to Eric," he snapped. "He's the one who needs it!"

"We all need Christ as our Savior, Bob," Danny replied softly.

His cousin strode into the kitchen and slammed the door.

That evening they all gathered in Mr. Orlis's room and had their family devotions. Danny's dad read the Bible, and then they took turns praying. That is, all except Bob. When they had finished, they sat quietly for a moment or two. Bob got to his feet, fidgeting nervously.

"Now you guys turn in," Mr. Orlis said, rumpling Danny's hair. "You've had a big day, and if this snow lets up tonight, you'll have a lot to do tomorrow."

The boys went up to Danny's room above the kitchen and got ready for bed.

"What do you make of all this?" Bob asked as they crawled in between the warm woolen blankets.

"I don't know what's going on," Danny told him. "I've never seen Dad and Tex this way before. But I can tell you this much. Whatever it is, it's awfully mysterious."

"And dangerous too," Bob added. "You should have seen the way Tex covered up his plane. And after staking it right next to the house, too. He really made sure nobody's going to find it."

They lay there for a moment or two, listening to the sound of the wind howling through the trees. And then they heard it. It was a faint sound at first, so faint that Danny couldn't be sure that he had heard anything at all. He rolled over on his side and lay there breathlessly—listening.

And then it came again, a little louder, but still muffled and indistinct.

"Did–did you hear that?" Bob whispered.

"I–I thought I heard something," Danny replied.

"What did it sound like?" Bob asked.

It came a third time from just outside their window, the unmistakable sound of a saw blade against high carbon steel.

"Somebody's at Tex's plane!" Danny Orlis cried, throwing off the covers and leaping out of bed. "Somebody's out there!"

CHAPTER 3

THE PLANE IS REPAIRED

"Come on, Bob!" Danny cried. "Somebody's out there fooling with Tex's plane!"

"In this storm?" Bob echoed as he scrambled out of bed and started to pull on his clothes. "It can't be!"

"But it is!" Danny said excitedly. "Hurry up or we'll be too late!"

Danny slipped into his jeans and boots, pulled on his parka, and was searching frantically for the flashlight which he knew was around the room somewhere, while Bob dressed hurriedly.

"Come on, Bob!" Danny said, snatching up the flashlight and starting toward the door. "Come on!"

"I'm right behind you!"

The wind was howling around the corner of the house and whistled in at the window, building a fine cone of snow on the icy window ledge and chilling the room with its breath. But Danny was too excited to be cold.

Bob grabbed up a baseball bat that he had seen standing in the corner earlier in the evening. "I'm right behind you, Danny!"

By this time the noise had awakened the rest of the household.

"Danny!" his mom called from the other part of the house. "What's wrong? What's going on up there?"

And from the guest bedroom Tex boomed, "What's the matter, Danny?"

But there wasn't time to answer them now. Danny and Bob went racing down the stairs, out into the kitchen, and flung open the outside door. A blast of white, swirling snow enveloped them.

Bob sucked in his breath sharply and took a step or two backward. "Nobody could even live in that!" he managed. "There's no one out there!"

"But there is!" Danny retorted. "There's got to be!"

With that Danny went plunging out the door into the soft, swirling, blinding snow. For an instant or two the fury of it snatched his breath away and stung his cheeks and hands. Then he steeled himself and stumbled toward the plane, his flashlight stabbing a tiny hole in the curtain of white that hung like a shroud about them.

"There's the plane!" Bob shouted in his ear as the light revealed the tip of one wing.

Danny straightened sharply, catching his breath. He hadn't even realized that Bob had come outside with him!

"You were right!" Bob cried. "Somebody's been here all right!"

A glance showed that that was true. The snow had been brushed off the wing, and the drift under it had been hurriedly pushed away. The big canvas which Tex had used to cover it had been slashed and ripped aside.

The boys struggled through the drifted snow to reach the light plane.

"Look!" Danny cried as he let the light run along the wing's trailing edge. There at the aileron the control cable had been half sawed through. And, sticking out of the snow beneath it, was the tip of a broken hacksaw blade.

"What do you know!" Bob exclaimed.

Tex had come up behind them and was standing there wordlessly.

"Just as I thought," he said at last. "I might have known they'd find it."

Danny stared at the half-cut cable. If they hadn't heard the guy during a momentary lull in the storm, Tex might not have noticed the almost severed cable! It could have cost him his life!

Back inside, Tex's usually kind face had grown dark.

"That settles it, Carl," he said quietly. "I'm going to get that sheriff to investigate this if I have to rope and hogtie him to get him out here."

Mrs. Orlis sent the two boys back upstairs to bed, but Tex borrowed Carl's deer rifle and sat beside the kitchen stove, the lamp on, and the gun across his knees.

"I hope he comes back," he muttered darkly. "I just hope he comes back!"

Danny and Bob, shivering, crawled back between the blankets.

"What do you make of that, Danny?" Bob whispered.

"Somebody's certainly out after Tex," Danny answered. He lay there for a long while listening to the howling wind. "And we've got to find out just who it is before something terrible does happen."

The boys lay there quietly after that, trying to sleep, but they could not. A thousand wild thoughts raced through their minds.

At breakfast the next morning nobody mentioned what had happened the night before, but Tex was strangely silent, and Danny noticed that his dad's face was pale and drawn.

It stopped snowing and blowing unexpectedly just before dawn, and the sun came out to bathe the snow-clad trees and lake in a dazzling brilliance that made Danny's eyes ache and sent him into the house after his sunglasses.

The two boys helped Tex scoop his plane out of the snow and repair the control cable, then stood silently while he warmed up the motor and took off into the cloudless blue sky.

All the while they worked, Tex said nothing until just before he climbed into his plane. Then he turned to Danny.

"You look after things," he said softly, "and keep a sharp eye out for strangers or anything odd or suspicious. I'll be back just as soon as I can get that sheriff pried away from his desk."

"I'll do my best," Danny said.

CHAPTER 4

THE INDIAN WOMAN
AND HER BABY

When the plane was in the air, Bob turned to Danny. "You know," he said, "whoever tried to sabotage Tex's plane last night must have done it once before. He must be the one who's responsible for your dad getting hurt."

Danny nodded solemnly. "That's the way I've got it figured," he said. "That's why we've got to hunt until we find him."

The two boys pitched into the work outside, scooping a narrow walk out to the post office behind the cabin, another to the barn, and still a third to the big woodpile which was stacked not far from the house. Then Danny hitched Laddie, the Southern Gentleman, his second-best dog, and the rest of his team to his improvised sled.

"We'll do a little scouting around," he said, "and see if we can find out anything."

They went over to Magnuson's Island and American Point with Bob sitting on the sled and Danny standing in back doing the driving, but they didn't see anything out of the ordinary.

"I haven't seen any strangers around at all, Danny," the postmaster at American Point told him. "Why?"

"We just thought we had a visitor last night," Danny said.

The next morning Tex and the sheriff came out and spent the day poking around and asking questions. But when the time came for them to go, they hadn't learned anything either.

"I don't know what to make of it," Mr. Orlis said after family devotions. "Neither the boys nor the sheriff and Tex were able to learn a thing. Nobody has seen any strangers around, and there surely isn't any reason for anybody who lives here to have it in for Tex. I don't believe he's got an enemy in the whole Angle country."

"Maybe whoever is doing it has gone away," Danny's mom said hopefully. "Maybe they were after somebody else."

Mr. Orlis did not answer.

The boys were so busy with their studies and the work around the post office that they had almost forgotten Christmas was approaching until Mrs. Orlis asked them to go out into the forest and cut a big tree.

"It's great to be up here for Christmas," Danny said as he picked out a tree that would be suitable. "It's really going to be some Christmas for all of us!"

"I don't know," Bob replied doubtfully. "I thought that we'd be able to get down to Warroad to do some Christmas shopping. I haven't bought a gift for anybody yet. It's certainly not going to be much of a Christmas for me."

"We can probably get into Warroad some day next week," Danny said, "if you feel like you want to give some things. But the gifts aren't important, really. The important thing is that Jesus came to earth to die and to rise from the grave so that you and I might be saved."

Bob stared at him strangely.

"We have a wonderful time at Christmas," Danny went on. "You just wait and see."

The days passed rapidly, and before they realized it, the day before Christmas Eve was upon them. Tex brought out a load of mail soon after sunup, and while Danny sorted and distributed it, the flier went back for the second load.

Most of the mail had been picked up when a swarthy, scowling Indian who towered half a head above the others came up to the window.

"Anything for me?" he demanded.

Danny fished a long, slender package out of the diminishing pile behind him.

"This is a funny shaped package," he said. And then he saw the rubber stamp on the wrapper. "A dozen hacksaw blades."

Hacksaw blades! Cold sweat broke out on Danny's forehead and the palms of his hands. Tex's plane had

had a hacksaw used on it the night before the big storm, and he had found a piece of broken hacksaw blade in the snow beneath the wing!

Somehow Danny managed to get all the mail distributed and closed the door to the post office.

"I'm going to get the dogs harnessed, Bob," he said. "You go and tell Mom that we'll be back soon."

It wasn't far across the lake to the place where the Indian had his muskrat camp. Danny had fished and hunted over there hundreds of times. Darkness had already settled over the Angle, but he headed straight for the crude log cabin where the Indian and his family lived.

"What are we going to do after we get there?" Bob asked.

"Snoop around a little," Danny answered, "and see if we can dig up any clues for the sheriff."

"We've got to be careful," Bob cautioned, lowering his voice. "Anybody who will try to do what he did to your dad and Tex is plenty dangerous."

They could see the lamplight through the window from a distance, but as they drew closer, Danny called softly to the dogs.

"There's something wrong over there," he said. "There's a light all right, but as cold as it is, there's no smoke coming from the chimney."

"Maybe the fire's gone down a little and we just can't see it," Bob said.

"No, sir," Danny replied firmly. "There's something wrong!"

They slipped up to the cabin as carefully and as quietly as they could until they could look in the smoky window.

"What do you know!" Danny exclaimed.

There on a little cot lay a young Indian mother, covered with a few thin rags. Her face was pale and twisted with pain. A tiny baby about two or three weeks old lay in a cradle close by. And above the woman hung a hacksaw with a broken blade.

"Do you see that?" Bob demanded hoarsely.

Danny nodded. He knew at a glance that the other half of the blade was in his pocket.

"Let's get out of here," Bob chattered.

"We can't," Danny whispered. "I'll go in and get a fire going. You'd better take the dog team and go back to our place and get Mom as quickly as you can!"

"But Danny!" Bob countered. "That guy'll kill you if he comes home and finds you here!"

"We can't leave her in there like that," Danny said. "She's sick and cold and probably hungry. Jesus says that we're supposed to look after the sick and the hungry just as we'd want others to do for us. We just can't leave her, Bob."

"But your mom wouldn't come over here to the home of the man who tried to kill your dad," Bob protested. "And even if she would, he wouldn't let her."

"Yes, he would," Danny said excitedly. "And Mom will come if you tell her about the woman and the baby. But hurry! That woman must be awfully sick!"

Bob shook his head doubtfully. "You mean that you're actually going in there a-a-and take the chance of–of getting yourself killed to help an Indian woman and her baby whom you've never seen before—the wife of the guy who tried to kill Tex and your dad?"

"You've got to get going, Bob!" Danny cried. "Hurry!"

For an instant Bob stood there. Then in a hushed voice he said, "Danny, if being a Christian will make a guy brave enough to do what you're going to do, I–I want to be a Christian too!"

"That's wonderful, Bob," Danny said as he started toward the cabin door.

"I–I just wanted to tell you, Danny," his cousin went on, "in case something happened to you before I get back."

CHAPTER 5

BIG JOHN COMES HOME

Bob stood there for a moment or two, staring hard at Danny.

"I–I'll be back just as soon as I can," he blurted. "Take care of yourself!" Then he whirled and ran back to the place where they had left the dog team.

"Come on, Laddie! Up!" he shouted. "Up, Southern Gentleman! Laddie! Let's go!" He snatched the whip and cracked it resoundingly in the still night air. "Mush, boys! Mush!"

Danny watched Bob streak across the snow toward the Orlis cabin on Pine Creek as the big, husky dogs lay into the harness. It would take an hour to make the trip across the bay, half an hour or so for his mom to get ready, and an hour to come back. Cold, icy fingers of fear squeezed his stomach into a hard knot and set his heart racing in his throat.

Danny knew Big John Bedean, the Indian who had tried to wreck the plane. Everyone on the Angle knew Big John and tried to stay out of his way if possible. A shudder rippled up Danny's spine. If the Indian came home and found him there, he didn't have to guess what would happen. There wasn't another temper like his in all the Angle country.

"What have I been thinking about?" Danny asked himself, staring quickly about in the darkness. He couldn't stay there! Not at Big John Bedean's house! He would run back into the muskeg to hide and wait until Bob and his mom got back. That was the only safe thing to do!

And then he heard the baby cry, a weak, plaintive little cry that sounded more like that of one of his kittens than a real, live baby. The poor little thing was probably cold and hungry.

Danny turned and looked through the window once more. The mother tried to get up, then fell back exhausted on the bed. She was too weak even to care for her little one! At that moment Danny knew what he had to do.

"O, God," he prayed. "Just give me the courage to go in a-a-and do what I can to help. And help me not to be afraid no matter what happens."

Then he started quickly toward the door. The instant he touched the doorknob, the Indian woman on the cot stirred.

"John," she called weakly. "John, is that you?"

"It isn't John," Danny called out as bravely as he could.

He stepped inside and shut the door, stomping the snow from his boots. It was bitterly cold inside. He could see his breath in the feeble lamplight, and there was a layer of ice on the water in the washbasin. It had been hours since there had been a fire in the ramshackle little cabin.

"Who are you?" the Indian mother demanded brokenly, raising on one elbow. "What do you want?" Her eyes were wide with terror and her frail shoulders were trembling.

"I'm Danny Orlis from across the bay," he said simply, hurrying over to the stove and opening it.

"Orlis?" she echoed. Her eyes narrowed and she almost spat out the name. "Get out of here! You've caused us enough trouble already! Now go away and leave us alone!"

Danny looked at her quickly. Now what could she mean by that? She couldn't possibly know him. He had never seen her in his life before, until ten minutes ago.

"I'm not going to hurt you," he said. "We were going past and saw that you had no fire and figured you were probably in trouble. So we stopped by to see." He shook down the stove and put some paper and kindling in. "Right now I'm going to get a fire started. It's awfully cold in here!"

The Indian woman lay stiffly on the cot, her gaze riveted to his every move as he built the fire and opened the draft.

"You leave us alone," she managed. "You've done enough to us already."

Instead of answering he turned toward the crude little crib where the baby lay. The woman raised on one elbow, struggling weakly to get to her feet.

"Don't you dare touch my baby," she said in broken English. "Big John will kill you if you do! Big John will kill you!"

"But I'm not going to hurt your baby," Danny protested. "I just want to help you if I can. You and the baby are both awfully sick."

Danny did not move for an instant or two, then he stepped quietly forward and touched the baby's tiny hand. It was cold and tinged with blue.

"This little guy's cold," he said, skinning out of his parka and spreading it across the crib. "There, that ought to warm you up a little until we get that fire going good."

The Indian woman started violently as Danny touched the child, but when she saw that he did not intend to hurt him, she settled back on the pillow, her thin blue lips trembling uncertainly.

"Big John said he be back," she said, swallowing hard. "He said he be back after mail time. But he didn't come, and he didn't come."

Danny saw that her breath was coming in short, hacking gasps, and her face was flushed with fever. He had seen his mom that way once. Tex had flown her down to the hospital at Rosseau where the doctors said that she had a bad case of pneumonia. Here he was, alone in the cabin with a sick woman and baby, and he didn't know what to do.

With a prayer in his heart he went over to the kitchen cabinet in one corner of the one-roomed cabin and found a can of soup and a few crackers. By this time the fire was crackling merrily as it sent the first faint glow of warmth out to drive the cold from the room.

"I'll open this and heat it for you," he said. "By that time perhaps Bob and Mom will be here."

She eyed him suspiciously. "What are they coming for?" she demanded. "Why they want to come over here?"

"To help take care of you and the baby," Danny replied. "Mom's awfully good at things like that."

The Indian woman started to speak, then stopped suddenly. "You mean she come over here at night to take care of *my* baby?" she asked, as though she could scarcely believe what she had heard. "You mean she come to take care of *my* baby?"

Danny nodded. The tears welled in the Indian woman's eyes. "Nobody ever treated us like that before," she said weakly. "Nobody–"

At that moment there was a faint sound outside, the sound of the wind, or perhaps the cautious step of a woodsman approaching the door. Someone who did not want to be heard!

Big John! Danny's lips scarcely formed the words as he straightened suddenly and whirled to face the cabin's only entrance.

The sound came again, faintly and indistinct, from just outside the door.

"Your mother, maybe?" the young Indian woman asked hopefully. "She comes?"

Danny shook his head. "Mom and Bob had to come from way across the bay, and it would take her a little time to get ready. Th-there hasn't been time for them to get here," he said numbly. "It must be–" His voice trailed away as the door rattled and slowly began to swing open.

CHAPTER 6

AS SIMPLE AS THAT

Danny was frozen with fear as the door swung open. For the space of a heartbeat he was motionless.

There, half on his knees at the door, was Big John Bedean, his ugly face twisted with pain. The Indian stared at him blankly. Then the strength seemed to ebb from him, and he sagged to the floor.

"Big John!" Danny shouted, running forward.

The Indian woman excitedly muttered something in Chippewa and tried to rise but dropped exhausted back to the cot. The baby started to cry.

"Here!" Danny said. "Let me help you!" Somehow he managed to pull and lift the Indian man into the cabin and get the door closed.

"What's wrong with him?" the Indian woman demanded. "What happen?"

Danny saw at a glance what had happened. The sweat was standing out on Big John Bedean's forehead, and his leg was twisted strangely under him.

"It's his leg," Danny said. "I think he must have broken it."

The Indian man gritted his teeth and nodded. He tried to speak, but his breath was too short, unconsciousness too close.

"Let's get that heavy coat off," Danny said, "and see if we can't get you fixed a little more comfortable." Hurriedly he unbuttoned the Indian's fleece-lined coat and removed it.

Big John made no move of protest. "I fall," he said at last after Danny had him lying on the cot. "I don't know how it happen, but I–I fall on the ice. I think maybe I never get back here." He stopped two or three times as he spoke, breathing heavily and wiping at the sweat on his forehead. "It hurts, I tell you," he gritted. "It hurts!"

"Mom will be here in a little while," Danny told him. "She'll know what to do about this leg of yours."

Big John turned slowly toward Danny. "You're that Orlis kid, aren't you?" he growled, as though he just realized who Danny was. "What are you doing here?"

"I just came in to help," he stammered. The color drained from his face as he saw the look in Big John's eyes—he saw the hatred drive the pain away.

"Your dad and Tex gave me trouble," he grated, pulling himself up on one elbow. "They got me arrested for trapping beaver last fall. I kill you!"

The big man was sitting up straight now and staring at Danny. He backed slowly away, his heart hammering wildly.

"No, Big John!" the Indian's wife cried. "He come and fix fire! He send for help! No! No!"

At that instant there was a noise outside the door. Big John turned quickly as Bob and Mrs. Orlis and two of the neighbor men came in.

"We got back just as fast as we could, Danny," Bob said. "Are you all right?"

The young woodsman grinned weakly. "I think so," he said.

Danny's mom examined the baby first, and then the little Indian mother, with the practical air of one who was used to emergencies.

"It looks like we'll have to get the whole family to the hospital right away," she said. "We'd better take them over to our place and radio for Tex to come up after them the first thing in the morning."

At the mention of the tall flier's name, Big John's face darkened angrily in spite of the pain.

Phil Creighton and his brother Jerry loaded the Indian family into the ice boat, leaving only Danny and Bob behind.

"We'll be back after you guys in the morning," Phil said.

"You don't need to come after us," Danny told him. "We'll wait until daylight and walk back."

When the ice boat was gone, Danny and Bob stood there together. "I was sure glad to see you when you came in just now," Danny said. "It was Big John who tried to wreck the plane all right."

Bob nodded. "As soon as I mentioned his name to your dad, he said that every piece to the puzzle fell into place. He and Tex came on Bedean trapping beaver out of season last fall, and the next afternoon the Canadian game warden picked him up. He swore that they had turned him in."

"I thought he was going to tear me apart when he found out who I was," Danny went on. "Was I scared!"

Bob walked over to the cot and sat down on the edge of it. For a long while he stared into the fire that roared in the wood burning stove.

"You know," Danny said at last, "you mentioned something to me just before you left to go and get Mom this evening. Do you remember what it was?"

Bob nodded slowly. "I said that I wanted to be a Christian," he answered evenly.

"It isn't enough just to want to be a Christian," Danny told him. "You've got to put your whole trust in Jesus to save you from sin."

"Would—would you explain that to me again, Danny?" he asked softly.

"Well, first of all," Danny went on, "we have to recognize that the Bible is true when it says that everybody is a sinner and needs a Savior. We've got to know in our hearts that that applies to us, too."

"I understand that part all right," Bob told him.

"Then we've got to believe that Jesus died on the cross and rose from the dead, and that He has the power to forgive us of the sin in our lives."

"I understand that, too," Bob replied.

"Then all you have to do," Danny concluded, "is to confess your sins and put your trust in Jesus to forgive your sins, and you're a Christian."

"You mean it's that simple?" Bob asked.

"It's the simplest thing in the world," Danny said.

After a moment Bob got down on his knees beside the cot. Danny knelt, too, and the older boy poured out his heart to God. When he finally looked up, his face was radiant.

CHAPTER 7

CHRISTMAS WITH NEW MEANING

Danny and Bob lay down on the little cot, but they didn't sleep much that night. The wind whistled in around the door and the windows of the little Indian cabin and seeped in between the logs to steal the warmth from the fire, keeping them shivering. Finally, they got up and sat on the side of the bed, wrapping the thin blankets around them in a desperate attempt to keep warm. "Why don't you put another chunk of wood on the fire, Bob?" Danny asked sleepily. "It's your turn."

"But I went out in the cold after the last armload," Bob protested. Nevertheless, he opened the stove and shoved in another piece of wood, standing a moment to warm his hands before the fire.

"Just imagine," he continued, "people have to live in places like this, and with little babies, too. It certainly isn't any wonder that they get sick."

Danny nodded. "I was thinking that myself," he said. "I guess we aren't really thankful enough for all the blessings that God has given us. Our parents aren't rich. I suppose a lot of people would say that we're poor because we certainly don't have any more money than we need. But we do have good, warm clothes to wear and plenty to eat and a nice, warm home to live in."

Bob came back to the cot and sat down. "You know, it's a funny thing, Danny," he said, "but I never used to appreciate that sort of stuff. I always felt like the world owed it to me, and I'd get awfully mad at Mom and Dad when I couldn't have everything I wanted. But when I see people living like this, it makes me terribly ashamed of myself."

Danny got up and walked to the window. The first faint dull streaks of dawn were tinting the horizon with light. In a few minutes the sun would be climbing determinedly over the trees.

"It's getting light, Bob," Danny said. "Perhaps we had better start hiking across the bay. My parents will be expecting us."

"Not half as much as I'm expecting breakfast," Bob grinned. "I can just taste your mom's hot cakes and syrup and cocoa right now."

It was only two or three miles across the bay to Danny's home, and the boys didn't lose any time on the way, but they were still on the lake between little McCoy and Pine Creek when Tex came winging out of the south, circled, and landed on the ice almost at the Orlis doorstep.

"Come on," Danny said, breaking into a run. "I'll race you to the plane!"

"Old Tex must have been waiting for daylight just like we were," Bob panted as he and Danny ran neck and neck across the ice.

"Well," Tex was saying to Mr. and Mrs. Orlis as the two boys burst into the front door. "The Bedean family had a mighty close call. Doc said that the mother and baby probably wouldn't have lived if they hadn't gotten medical attention when they did."

"It was dangerous flying them out at night like you did," Mr. Orlis said.

"It had to be done," Tex said shortly.

"Well, I'm so relieved that you did get them there safely," Mrs. Orlis replied, "and that they're going to get along all right. I worried about them all night long."

"Big John's got a broken ankle," the flier continued. "But he's going to be okay, too." He took off his coat and sat down at the breakfast table. "What are we going to do about him, Carl? Are we going to bring charges against him for causing us to crash?"

"He's got his wife and baby to take care of," Mr. Orlis answered. "And I think he's learned his lesson. I'd just as soon let the matter drop."

"So would I," the flier said, "unless the insurance company insists on taking action."

Mr. Orlis turned to Danny. "You boys will want

to go into Warroad tomorrow to do some shopping," he said. "Why don't you stop at the hospital and tell Big John and his wife what we've decided. They're probably worrying terribly about it."

"Okay," Danny said.

After their shopping was completed, they went up to the hospital. Big John didn't say much, but he grasped Danny's hand and squeezed it hard.

"You boys got one good friend on the Angle," he choked. "Any time Big John can help, just let me know. Even if your dad send me to jail. I'm still your friend."

"But that's why we stopped to see you," Danny replied. "Dad and Tex decided yesterday that they weren't going to bring charges against you unless Tex's insurance company makes them."

"They–they're not?" Big John repeated.

"That's what they said," Danny answered.

"But I wrecked the plane. I–I could have killed them. And if I had, I–I'd have been glad about it. I was that mad." He shook his head. "I can't understand it. Nothing like this ever happened to me before."

"They figured that you'd learned your lesson," Danny said. "And they didn't want to take you away from your family."

Big John's face grew thoughtful. "Nobody ever treated me like that before," he said slowly. "I just can't figure it out. Nobody ever treated me like that before."

"It's because they are both Christian men," Bob put in suddenly. "I didn't know what a difference that makes until the other night when I–when I–" he stopped for a moment and gulped hard, "when I finally gave my heart to Christ."

For a long while Big John didn't speak at all, and when he did, Danny thought he could detect a slight tremor in the Indian's voice.

"Everybody say that Carl Orlis is different," he said at last. "But I never believe them. Now I know."

The boys wanted to keep on talking with him, but the nurse came in just then. They said goodbye to Big John and quickly made their way down the stairs.

Lugging their packages, they hiked out to the road where they caught a ride back to the house.

It seemed that Christmas was more wonderful than ever that year. They opened their packages on Christmas Eve after Mr. Orlis read the story of Christ's birth from the Book of Luke. And early Christmas morning they trudged through the snow to the little schoolhouse for services.

"I don't believe I ever spent a better Christmas," Bob said contentedly as he stretched out before the fireplace after dinner. "There's been so much about it that makes a guy feel so close to God."

"That's the way every Christmas ought to be," Mr. Orlis put in slowly.

The rest of the week raced past before they realized it. New Year's Day came and went and it was time for Bob and Danny to go back to Iron Mountain.

"I certainly hate to think about getting back to school," Danny said that last evening at home. "It seems like we just got here."

"I'll say," Bob echoed.

Nevertheless, the boys had their bags packed and were ready to leave when Tex came back for them the next morning. They got into Bemidji in time to catch the plane for Minneapolis, and it seemed only an hour or two until they were in the big Denver-bound jet high above southern Minnesota.

"I can't get Big John out of my mind," Bob said. "I certainly wish that we could have stayed and talked with him. He acted as though he had never heard about Jesus before. And he seemed to be so interested."

"There are a good many Indians up around the Angle who have never heard the Gospel," Danny said. "I don't know how long it has been since a missionary came up to work among them, but I guess it's been years and years and years."

"It makes a guy feel like learning the language and going to them, doesn't it?" Bob asked. "I never realized that there are people right here in America and Canada who have never heard about Jesus and how He died for their sins."

"They all aren't Indians either," Danny replied.

SECOND STRING FORWARD

CHAPTER 1

MIDWAY CAME A THREAT

When Danny Orlis and Bob got off the plane, Uncle Claude, Aunt Lydia, and Larry all came out of the air terminal to meet them.

"Hey, are we ever glad to see you guys!" Larry exclaimed, picking up Danny's suitcase and starting toward the car.

"Now what's up?" Danny questioned.

"It's tragic, I tell you," Larry went on. "We've played three basketball games and lost them all."

"That *is* rough," Danny said. "What's the trouble? I thought we were supposed to have a good team this year."

"We would have if we had any height," Larry went on. "You and Bob are the only tall guys on the squad. The guys are fast and can shoot and handle the ball, but we've got to have a tall guy or two in there to help control the tip-offs."

Danny Orlis looked over at Bob and grinned. Basketball was just about his favorite sport.

The next morning Danny had no sooner stepped inside the school building than Coach Edwards sent for him and had him pick up a uniform.

"I've never seen you play basketball," he said, "but from the way you handle a football I've got high hopes."

"I'll do my best," promised Danny.

"I know you will. It might be that we'll be counting on you to take Eric's place. I'd been planning to build my whole basketball team around him this year before that gambling mess broke."

"What did they do to Eric, Coach?" Danny asked. It was strange, but he hadn't even thought about Eric Tanner for weeks—not since he and Bob had left Iron Mountain to go up to the Angle.

"Well, when he got out of the hospital, they held his trial," the coach went on. "And he's in the detention center now. You might be interested in knowing that it was yours and Larry's testimony that sent him there. That affidavit you gave the sheriff and county attorney before you left helped to do the trick."

The smile faded from Danny's face. "I–I'm sorry about that," he said. "I certainly didn't want to help s-send him there."

Coach Edwards looked at the boy strangely. "I don't know why not," he said. "Eric certainly got just exactly what he deserved."

That evening after school Danny went out for his first basketball practice. He had only played the game on a regular court a few times, but he had a hoop up on the barn back home and had practiced shooting baskets by the hour. Coach Edwards put him with the reserves to scrimmage against the first team.

It seemed odd to be playing on a wooden floor after having played for so long on the grass. The ball bounced higher and faster, and several times he let it get away from him. He could feel the coach watching him, and the color rose slowly to his cheeks.

Midway in the second quarter Duke Millington, a short, stocky friend of Eric Tanner's, came in to play opposite the young woodsman.

"Hi, Duke," Danny smiled.

Duke swore at him and turned away.

On the first jump ball between them, Duke kneed Danny viciously in the stomach.

"Take it easy, Duke," Danny said to him.

"Listen, Orlis," Duke Millington snarled. "You did a friend of mine wrong. You squealed on him. And I'm going to get even." He stared with savage anger at Danny. "And it won't be a little knee in the stomach, either. I'll really get even!"

Danny wasn't afraid of Duke, but for some reason the cold shivers went racing up his spine.

CHAPTER 2

YOUTH GROUP GETS A RECRUIT

Danny, Larry, and Bob went out for basketball practice every night after school. Bob, who had lettered the year before, was on the varsity, and Larry played with the second string.

"Frankly, Danny," Coach Edwards said after the third or fourth practice session, "I don't know what to do with you. You're a dead eye at the basket, but you dribble as though you were pitching hay."

"I've never played on anything but grass before," Danny told him. "I've got a hoop at home where I practice a lot, just for fun, but I really have to slug the ball hard in order to dribble. Now every time I try, the ball bounces over my head."

"You wouldn't have to dribble as hard even though you were ten feet tall," the coach laughed. "I want you to practice dribbling and handling the ball, Danny.

We need your sharpshooting at the basket, but you'll have to master those two things if you're going to be able to help us much."

"I know that," Danny replied. "I'll certainly do my best."

Danny and Larry started practicing handling and dribbling in the basement at home, and the next week the coach assigned Danny temporarily to the second string.

"You'll get a chance to play more," the coach explained, "and get to handle the ball and dribble in action."

"That's great," Danny told him. "I don't care where I play, just so I get to play."

"I'm still counting on you at that forward spot on the varsity," the coach added softly.

For an instant Danny Orlis grinned. And then the smile faded quickly. He knew which forward Coach Edwards was expecting him to replace. He had seen the frown on the instructor's face when Duke went charging toward the basket with the ball or used his knees or elbows on the opposition.

That afternoon, when the reserves lined up to scrimmage with the regulars, Duke Millington sauntered arrogantly up to Danny.

"Down with the scrubs now, I see," he said belligerently.

"That's right," answered Danny.

"I thought you were going to burn up the league," he went on.

"You must be thinking about two other guys," Danny told him pleasantly.

"If you get in my way, it'll be too bad for you," Duke threatened. "I haven't forgotten what you did to Eric, and I'm going to get even with you."

Just then Coach Edwards blew the whistle sharply. "All right, guys," he called loudly, "let's play ball."

"Don't forget what I said," Duke cautioned under his breath as he moved back into his position.

* * * *

Danny Orlis was pleased that first Thursday night when Bob announced that he was going to youth group. They had never been able to get him to go there before.

Bob sat on the edge of his chair that first meeting, his Bible open on his lap. And when it was over, he hung around until almost everyone else had gone home in order to ask some questions of the speaker.

"You know, Danny," Bob said when they finally started home. "I used to think you and Larry were big sissies to go to church every Thursday night, but now I see that I was the sissy. I just didn't know what I was missing."

"I know just what you mean," Danny told him. "It takes the best a guy has to follow Jesus."

They walked a block or two in silence. "The pastor, Mr. Johnson, said that I ought to start reading the Bible," Bob went on thoughtfully. "I promised him I would."

"That's great," answered Danny. "The Bible has the answer to all our problems if we'll just read it and do what it tells us."

On Friday evening Danny played his first game of basketball before a crowd. Coach Edwards started him at forward with the second team and let him play all of the first half and most of the second in spite of his clumsiness.

It was even harder to hang onto the ball with the gym full of spectators and the opposing players darting toward him, waving their arms and trying to snatch the ball away. He had trouble making the ball and his feet behave at the same time, and the first three occasions he got the ball, it was taken from him for traveling.

"Take it easy, Danny," Larry whispered as the crowd laughed at the way he bungled a play. "Just take it easy. This isn't any different from playing in our basement at home. Only here we've got an audience."

The young woodsman grinned at him and relaxed a little. It was good to have a friend out on the floor with him—someone who wasn't laughing at him.

He settled down for a few minutes and somehow managed to work into position to shoot. It was at a bad angle, but the ball swooshed through the hoop so cleanly that the crowd gasped.

"That's the stuff," Larry called across the floor to him. "That's the way to show 'em."

A moment later Danny took the ball again and sent another looping shot through the basket without even touching the rim. There was a roar of approval from the crowd, but Danny scarcely heard them as he dropped back into his defensive position. This was something else he didn't know very much about, this worrying about a dribbler and trying to snatch the ball away or guarding a man as he went to pass or shoot.

Finally, however, the game was over and in the dressing room Coach Edwards called Danny aside.

"You did all right out there tonight, Orlis," he said. "I was proud of you."

"Thanks, Coach," he replied.

"Keep working on that ball handling, though," the coach cautioned. "You're going to have to learn a lot more basketball before you'll be able to do us much good on the varsity."

Danny hurried into a shower and dressed quickly so that he wouldn't miss any of the varsity game.

CHAPTER 3

QUESTIONS AND A TROUBLEMAKER

Both teams were victorious that night, and Danny and Larry celebrated with a malt down at Hammond's. When they got home, Bob came to the doorway of Danny's room and called to them.

"Come here a minute, guys," he said. "I've got a couple of things I want to ask you about."

"Sure thing," Danny answered.

"That was a terrific game you played tonight, Bob," Larry said as they went into his brother's room and shut the door. "You were red-hot."

"We were plenty lucky," Bob replied. Then he picked up his Bible and turned to Danny. "You know I promised the pastor that I'd start reading my Bible," he said suddenly.

Danny nodded.

"Well, I started tonight," the older boy said, "and there are some things here that I just can't understand."

"There are a lot of things in the Bible that I can't understand," Larry said easily. "When you come to something like that, you've just got to trust."

But that answer didn't satisfy his brother. "Just the same," he went on, "I've got to get an answer to this—one that satisfies me."

"What's giving you trouble, Bob?" Danny asked him. "Maybe we can help you."

"Well," Bob said, opening to the first chapter of Genesis, "it says here that God created the heavens and the earth and the animals and even people."

"That's right," Danny answered.

"But everybody knows that the world just evolved," Bob protested. "Life started from the little amoeba and kept changing and changing and changing down through millions of years until we've finally got animals and birds and people and fish and everything just the way we see them today."

For a couple of minutes Danny didn't say anything. "I don't know just how to explain it," he said frankly. "But I do know that what the Bible says is true."

Bob got up and walked across the room and back again. There was a serious frown on his face. "I don't know how you can say that," he repeated. "Look at all of our biology and zoology books. The people who write them know what they're talking about. They have to!"

"I've never studied either subject very much," Danny countered. "But the Bible is God's Word. Everything that is in it is true. So, if anything in these books you mention is different from the Bible, then the books are wrong. They've got to be."

Bob opened his Bible thoughtfully for a moment or two, then closed it and looked up at Danny.

"I'm going to talk to our biology teacher about this," he said at last. "I–I want to believe that the Bible is true, that it's really God's Word, but I–I just don't see how they can both be right. And the scientists have certainly got the evidence to prove that they are correct." His voice trailed away uncertainly.

Danny did not answer him.

"I know that stuff isn't true," Danny said to Larry when they were alone together in his basement room. "But I've never studied it, and I just didn't know what to say."

"I didn't either," Larry agreed. "Bob always has been a brain on science–ever since he was a little kid. I think he's read everything like that he could get his hands on."

"I certainly hope he gets straightened out," Danny said. "It scares me a little to hear him doubting the Bible that way when he's been a Christian for such a short while. He might get 'way off the track."

The next afternoon after school Coach Edwards put Danny with the varsity.

"I'm going to practice you here for a while," he explained. "I want you to play with some boys who are a little better skilled at ball handling. We need your sharpshooting on the first string if you can just master the fundamentals of the game."

Duke turned to Danny and glared at him.

The coach divided the squad into two teams and scrimmaged them against each other. By chance Danny and Duke were on the same team.

"You don't need to think that you're so good, Snitch," Duke muttered under his breath. "You aren't going to last long with the first string."

Every time Duke could rifle Danny a bad pass without being seen, he did so. The ball bounced off the young woodsman's fingertips or scooted between his legs or sometimes just missed him altogether.

"What's the matter, Orlis?" Coach Edwards asked during one of the frequent time outs. "You're handling the ball worse than you did the other night."

Danny could feel his cheeks coloring. "I'll try to do better," he said.

"You'll have to," the coach replied shortly.

Out on the floor once more Duke turned to Danny again. "I don't know why you keep on coming out for basketball," he gloated. "You haven't got a chance of making the varsity."

Danny managed a weak little grin and turned away. He knew how true Duke's words could be.

CHAPTER 4

THE TEAM AND PEGGY BOTH WIN

Coach Edwards was shuffling the teams around night after night, trying to find the best combinations, but Danny and Larry were still on the second team. In the evenings, if they didn't have homework to do or youth group to attend, they went down into the basement at home and practiced dribbling and passing. "You're getting it a little better now," Larry panted one evening as they stopped a moment to rest. "The way you can shoot you'll be on the first team before you know it."

"I'm not so sure," Danny said uncertainly. "I still don't feel at all sure of myself on the court. And I can't begin to hold onto the sort of passes that Duke sends my way."

"You ought to tell him off," Larry said, his eyes snapping. "That's what I'd do if I were you. He doesn't throw to anyone else that way."

"I think it's on account of Eric," Danny answered. "They used my affidavit at his trial. Duke says that he's going to get even with me for it. He says that it's my fault that Eric is in the detention center, that he'd have gone free if it hadn't been for me."

"All you did was to tell the truth," Larry replied, "the same as I did. The next time he throws to you like that why don't you complain to Coach Edwards. He'd really clobber him."

Danny shook his head. "Nope," he said. "I can't do that. What I've got to do is to learn to catch passes like that. Throw me a couple of hard ones, will you, Larry?"

Danny kept working as hard as he could at dribbling and handling the ball, but somehow he didn't seem to get the knack of it. He had been bouncing a basketball on the grass up at Angle Inlet too long for it to come easily to him.

Duke didn't help things either. After a few days with the varsity, Coach Edwards put him on the second team, too, and Danny found himself playing with him. At every opportunity Duke Millington burned those hard passes at the young woodsman.

"I was in hopes that you'd be ready to play with the varsity, Danny," Coach Edwards said at the close of the last practice session before the game with Madison. "But you don't seem to be getting the hang of handling the ball like you should. What's the matter? Aren't you practicing at home the way I asked you to?"

"Larry and I have been practicing every chance we get," Danny answered.

"Well," the coach concluded, "you're going to have to play with the second team until you learn how to handle the ball."

Danny flushed red but said nothing.

Danny started at forward with the second team against Madison. From the moment he went out onto the floor he knew that he was going to have a good night. The basketball felt light and sure in his hands, and he was as relaxed and at ease as though he was only practicing in the basement at home.

On the opening play he took the ball from the fingers of a Madison man, faked around him, and dribbled in for a clean, looping basket. Moments later he broke up a Madison play under the goal by leaping into the air and coming down with the ball.

"Danny," Coach Edwards said seriously, "if you could just learn to dribble and handle the ball, you'd be one of the regulars on the first string, and we'd stand a lot better chance in the Conference."

The second team won their game that night by a sizable margin, and the varsity managed to squeak through to victory in the final game. The guys were laughing and talking happily as they took their showers and changed clothes.

* * * *

The youth group at church usually met on Thursday night, but they planned a special program for after the service on Sunday evening, and Bob went with Larry and Danny.

"You know," he said as they entered the basement and took seats well up front, "if someone would have told me a couple of months ago that I'd be going to something like this on a Sunday night, I'd have told them they were crazy."

"I was the same way before I trusted Christ as my Savior," Larry said softly. "But now I think I was crazy for ever doing anything else on Sunday night."

Peggy came in just then. She caught Danny's eye and smiled and waved to him.

"Hi, there," he said, grinning back. It was the first time that he had seen her since she got out of the hospital. "I didn't know that you'd be here tonight."

"It's so good to be back in church," she said. "It seems as though I've been gone for ages and ages."

That evening the discussion seemed to get away from the leader. The kids began to talk about dating and whether or not Christians should ever date those who are unsaved.

"I don't see what difference it makes," Bob put in. "We've got to have someone to run around with, whether we're Christian or not. The fact is, I think that a Christian guy or girl might be able to convert his date to Christ by setting a good example. I don't think that we need to draw ourselves off into a little corner just because we've trusted Christ as our Savior."

Peggy got quickly to her feet. Her pale face was serious, and Danny thought he saw a tear glistening in a corner of her eye.

"I don't think that we ought to draw ourselves off into a little corner," she agreed, "just because we have accepted Christ as our personal Savior, but you are all wrong about dating unsaved kids. I know." She stopped for a moment, biting her lip.

"I was going out with Eric when I became a Christian, and I–I just didn't see how I could possibly give him up. I tried to fool myself that I was going to convert him to Christ, but every time I went out with him, I found myself compromising my faith. I–I'd go to a show with Eric so that he'd go to church with me. I'd go to a dance if he'd go to youth group. I was miserable all the time. And–and then we had the accident and–and" She swallowed hard, "you all know what happened after that."

She stopped again, and it was so quiet in the church basement that they could hear the clock ticking in the next room.

"Finally, after the accident I knew that I had to give him up," she continued when she could speak again. "It was awfully hard, but you'll never know how relieved I am now, and happy too. And I'm never going anywhere–not even out walking–with another guy who hasn't accepted Christ as his Savior."

For a long while nobody spoke. Then Bob said, "I guess that is right, Peggy. I had never thought of it quite that way before."

CHAPTER 5

DANNY FACES THE SCIENTIFIC APPROACH

At basketball practice Monday afternoon, the coach put the second team squad through tough drills.

At the opening of the scrimmage, Danny took the ball on the tip at center, and he and Duke went racing down the sidelines together. Danny whipped the ball to Duke and Duke rifled it back, a blistering throw just at Danny's fingertips. Coach Edwards blasted on his whistle.

"Duke!" he snapped. "There isn't a man on the first team who could catch a pass like that. What's the idea of smoking the ball at Danny? Didn't you want him to catch it?"

Duke flushed deeply but said nothing.

The coach turned to Danny. "I've been watching you so closely when you're on the floor," he said, "that I haven't been paying attention to the passes you've been getting. Has Duke been throwing that way to you all the time? Is that why you've been muffing the ball?"

"I don't think that's the only reason," Danny said truthfully.

Coach Edwards stroked his chin for a moment or two. "That might explain a lot of things," he muttered to himself. Then he turned to Duke. "I had been planning to start you with the second string this week. Now I'm going to give Danny his chance."

Danny felt the color drain from his face as the guys turned to look at him. Duke's lips were quivering with anger as he muttered under his breath. If the coach heard him, he said nothing.

"And another thing," Coach Edwards went on. "While I'm talking to you, I'd just as well get something else across." He stopped and looked over the squad thoughtfully. "Word has come to me that some of you guys have been smoking. If I catch any one of you smoking—I don't care who it is or how valuable to the team he is—he's going to be kicked off the squad. Do you understand?"

They all nodded gravely.

When the coach had finished and sent them to the showers, Duke sidled up to Danny.

"I'll get you yet," he muttered darkly. "Just wait. I'll get even with you!"

On the way to school the next morning Bob said to Danny, "I've got an appointment with Mr. Hanson, our biology teacher. I want to talk to him about fossils and evolution and things like that and see how they agree or disagree with the Bible. Do you want to come along?"

Danny hesitated. He had some studying that he ought to do. It was hard to keep his grades up and play basketball too. But he also ought to go with Bob.

Bob was such a new Christian and took so much stock in what anyone who claimed to be an authority had to say about science and things like that.

"Sure thing," he answered.

When the biology instructor learned why the two boys had come to see him, he leaned forward earnestly. "I don't know that I would dare to go this far in class," he said, "but you've come to me to ask about these things, and it would be dishonest of me not to give you my considered opinion."

He stopped and smiled crookedly. "Everyone knows that there is no truth whatever in those Old Testament legends concerning the Creation. Every civilization has wondered about the origin of the earth and man. They've all dreamed up some weird stories to explain it. But the evidence to disprove them is all around us. And nobody who is truly educated puts any real stock in them."

Danny saw doubt creep into Bob's face.

"I believe the Bible," Danny said, "and the story of Creation in Genesis. It's God's Word. It has got to be true."

The teacher looked at him. "Your parents believe it, too, don't they?"

He nodded. "Mom and Dad are both Christians."

"That's just the trouble," he said. "Misinformed, uneducated parents pass those legends on to their children as truth. It makes our task a great deal more difficult."

The young woodsman was stung by the charge but said nothing.

The teacher opened a drawer in his desk and took out his schedule for the coming semester.

"I'd like to have both of you boys enroll in one of my classes," he said. "I can't go into all of these things with you now, and I certainly don't want to argue with you about what you believe. But I would like to expose you to a scientific approach to Creation and the origin of man."

"I don't know," Danny said uncertainly. "I've got an awfully full schedule, and I'm trying out for basketball, too. I don't want to carry too big a load."

"I'd like to," Bob put in. "I've got to think these things through. I've got to have them settled in my mind."

"That's fine," Mr. Hanson said.

He turned to Danny.

"What's the matter?" he asked. "Are you afraid that Genesis won't stand up under a bit of scrutiny?"

"No," Danny replied. "I'm not afraid that what I believe won't stand up against any teaching such as evolution. And I'd like to take biology." He stopped a moment, weighing his words. "But I don't want to be in a class where I'll be laughed at and made fun of for what I believe."

The smile disappeared from Mr. Hanson's face. For a long time he sat there, staring past Danny and Bob.

Then he said, "I'll tell you what I'll do, Danny. I'll promise you that if you enroll in my class, we'll take the subject straight. I won't ridicule you for what you believe, and you won't ridicule me for what I believe. How's that?"

CHAPTER 6

THE COACH GIVES HIS ULTIMATUM

During the next two practice sessions, Coach Edwards had Danny practicing with the second team's starting five while Duke sat on the sidelines, glowering with rage.

"You're handling the ball better now, Orlis," Coach Edwards said at the close of the final session before the Lewisville game. "I believe you're coming along at last."

Danny said nothing. It was true that he had been doing better since the coach put someone else in Duke's spot at forward. Before that, he had always been tense and on edge, knowing that Duke would rifle the ball his way at a time when he least expected it. Now he could relax and concentrate on other things.

"Only watch your dribbling," the coach went on. "A sharp referee is very apt to call you for traveling the way you roll the ball in your hands as you dribble."

"I've been working on that," Danny told him.

"Fine."

The next evening as he and his cousins started for the gym, Larry said, "I don't know what's the matter with Coach Edwards. You ought to be playing on the first team, Danny."

"That's what I think," Bob agreed. "Why, there isn't one of us on the varsity who can begin to shoot like you can."

"I don't know about that," Danny said, "but I do know that I've got a lot to learn about handling the ball and dribbling. I think I'm lucky to be on the second team."

They were a little early getting to the gym, but some of the guys were already in the locker room. They could hear them talking as they walked downstairs.

"I just want to know one thing, Coach," Duke was saying angrily. "Is that baby, Danny Orlis, starting the game tonight, or am I?"

"You know that I don't make a habit of announcing my starting lineups before game time, Duke," Coach Edwards said evenly.

"If I don't get to play tonight, I'm turning in my uniform," Duke retorted, his temper rising. "That's what I'm going to do."

There was a long silence. Then the coach said, "You shouldn't make an ultimatum, Duke. You know that you're not so good that you can tell me whom I can play and whom I can't."

"There are a lot of guys who feel the same as I do," Duke went on. "They're plenty fed up with this guy coming in here from somewhere else and preaching at us—then getting to play regular when he'd never even been on a basketball court before this year."

"That's enough, Duke," Coach Edwards said softly.

At that Duke came storming out the door. When he saw Danny on the steps, he stopped.

"You'd better go in and put your uniform on, Sucker," he snarled under his breath, "and while you're at it, you can put mine on, too."

With that he pushed past them and went on outside.

Although Duke had threatened to quit the squad, he came wandering back into the dressing room just before the second team went on the floor and got into his uniform.

Coach Edwards acted as though nothing had happened between himself and the angry basketball player. He laughed and talked with him just as he did with the others. However, when the game started, Duke was on the sidelines. And on the sidelines he stayed, even though Iron Mountain forged far ahead, and Coach Edwards used his reserves for almost half the game.

Danny played well enough that night. Not spectacularly, but well enough to satisfy Coach Edwards.

"You're doing all right, fella," the coach said, looping his arm over Danny's shoulder as they walked back to the dressing room. "Just keep plugging away, and we'll get your ball handling troubles ironed out yet."

In the locker room, however, Coach Edwards called the guys together once more before he went back to the floor with the first team.

"You guys did all right," he said, "but I don't want you to think that you're so good you can knock off everyone that way. You were playing a weak team. We're going to have to keep hammering on fundamentals and working as hard as we can if we're to keep on winning." He stopped for a moment or two and looked over the squad, his eyes narrowing.

"And another thing," he went on at last. "I've warned you all about smoking, but evidently some of you aren't paying any attention to what I've been saying. I've found a little evidence that some of you are breaking training by smoking. I've heard rumors, too. I want to warn you for one last time that if I catch you, either with cigarettes or smoking, I'm going to dismiss you from the team for the season. Do you all understand that?" The hot little room was breathlessly quiet.

CHAPTER 7

IN THE BIBLE OR IN THE ROCKS

Danny and Bob and Larry finally got things arranged so that they could enroll in Mr. Hanson's biology class. They had to see the principal and make arrangements to switch one of their other classes. The biology sessions started out like any other class, and Danny and Larry began to feel a little better about taking the subject. "I think Mr. Hanson must have been kidding you guys," Larry said. "He hasn't said a word about evolution, the Bible, or anything like that. And his lessons have certainly been on the ball."

"I'm beginning to think the same thing," Danny told him.

However, it wasn't long until the course of the lessons changed abruptly. One afternoon during the following week, Mr. Hanson leaned back in his chair and stared straight at Danny Orlis.

"Our lesson today takes up some things that by their very nature are controversial," he began. "We're going to begin a study of the rocks and fossils and the probable origin of man."

Danny looked at Bob. His cousin was leaning forward, listening intently.

"We aren't going to deal with the big words now," Mr. Hanson went on. "So we won't touch on the names of the various ages. However, you will find that there are several distinct and separate ages that have left their proof in the rocks. The earliest age, which is millions upon millions of years old, has no fossils at all in the rock strata. The next age is depicted by rocks which have the fossils of invertebrates, the earliest known form of life."

Mr. Hanson continued with his outline of the order of Creation as he saw it, but Danny's mind wandered. He looked over at Bob. His cousin was hanging eagerly on every word. Danny knew what he was thinking. He was comparing what Mr. Hanson was saying with what the Bible said.

"How could Genesis be right," Bob would be asking himself, "when the rocks proved that the world had evolved, and all of life on the world had evolved down through millions and millions of years? How could man have been created as the Bible said he was when science had found that the story of evolution, the very history of it, was recorded in the rocks?"

Danny knew that what Mr. Hanson was saying couldn't all be true because it was only theory, and the Bible was the Word of God. But Bob was another matter.

As soon as the class session was over, Bob went up to the front of the room to talk further with the teacher, while Larry and Danny got their books together.

"I've never been in such an interesting class, Mr. Hanson," they heard Bob say as they went out.

"Wow!" Larry exclaimed. "What do you make of that?"

Danny shook his head. "I just don't know," he said thoughtfully. "It's not going to hurt my faith any. I don't know all the answers to that stuff, but I do know that the Bible is the Word of God, and there aren't any people who can prove that it's wrong."

"It isn't going to hurt me, either," Larry said determinedly. "At least I've been praying and praying that it wouldn't. But I'm not so sure about Bob. He's so wrapped up in science and anything scientific that he seems to swallow everything Mr. Hanson says."

"I know it," Danny agreed.

They walked to the end of the hall in silence.

"It makes me so mad just thinking of it," Larry blurted suddenly, "that I feel like getting up in class and telling Mr. Hanson where to get off."

"That won't do any good," Danny told him.

Larry acted as though he hadn't even heard him.

"I know what I'm going to do," he went on. "I'm going to get one of those books that gives the Bible's side to things like evolution and fossils and stuff—a book that's written by a real authority. I'm going to read up on it and give Mr. Hanson a bad time. He'll wish he had never brought the subject up."

"I feel the same way you do about evolution," Danny replied, "or anything else that attacks the Bible as God's Word. But it wouldn't do any good for us to attack Mr. Hanson. That would only make him mad. And we couldn't blame him. He's our teacher. We've got to show our respect for him as such. And you've got to give him credit for it, he hasn't brought the Bible into class the way I thought he would. He's kept his word on that."

"But he might just as well bring it in," Larry answered. "He's doing just as much harm as if he did. It makes me so mad to sit there and have to listen to that junk."

"This is something that we can't work out alone," Danny said slowly. "It's something that we're going to have to pray about a lot and be awfully careful of what we do or say. We've got to help Bob keep his faith in the Bible, that it is God's Word. But we want to be sure that we don't go about it in the wrong way."

"I can't see that," Larry retorted. "I'd think that any way we could help him would be all right."

"No," Danny countered, "we can't do wrong ourselves, even to help Bob, and expect God to bless our efforts."

That night when they got home from school, they talked with Larry's brother about it.

"I want to believe the Bible," Bob said. "Honestly I do. But–" he gulped hard—"but it seems strange to me that all of these people who have really studied—the scientists and biologists and people like that—all believe the way Mr. Hanson does–"

Danny looked quickly at Larry. Fingers of ice seemed to clutch his heart again.

* * * *

The next night they played Norwood. The three boys ate a light supper and went over to the gym early.

"I certainly hope that none of the guys have been smoking," Bob said. "Coach Edwards wasn't kidding when he said that he'd kick them off the team if he caught them."

"I know it," Danny answered.

Half the team was already in the locker room when the three of them entered. Danny went over to his locker and jerked an old jacket out to get at his basketball .

As he did so, a package of cigarettes slipped out of the pocket and fell on the floor, almost at Coach Edwards' feet.

Conversation choked off. Every eye in the room was riveted on the telltale cigarettes and Danny. He felt the color leave from his cheeks and the sweat stand out on his forehead.

CHAPTER 8

A REPUTATION IS WORTH SOMETHING

For two full minutes the dressing room was breathlessly quiet. Everyone stared down at the cigarettes on the floor and then up at Danny and Coach Edwards.

"I–I–" he stammered, trying to find the words to tell Coach Edwards that the cigarettes weren't his, that he had never seen them before. But as he began to speak, his tongue thickened, and his voice trailed away miserably.

The coach slowly took a step or two forward, stopped, and picked up the cigarettes. He fingered the half-filled pack for an instant. All the while he stared straight into Danny's eyes.

"Are these yours, Orlis?" he asked quietly, holding them in his hand. "Do they belong to you?"

There was a long silence. Then Duke broke in angrily. "Of course, they're his. Who else would be keeping cigarettes in Danny's pockets?"

"Are they yours?" the coach asked again, ignoring Duke.

Danny shook his head.

"No, they're not," he replied simply. "I know that it sounds strange, but I never saw them before. I don't have the slightest idea how they got there."

The coach stood there for a moment, biting his lower lip thoughtfully. Then he turned to Bob and Larry.

"Have either of you guys ever seen Danny smoke?" he asked.

They shook their heads.

"No," Larry said. "I know that he doesn't smoke. He lives at our place. We'd know it if he did."

"What did you expect him to say?" Duke demanded angrily. "Danny's his own cousin. He'd lie for him."

Larry started to protest, but Coach Edwards cut in sharply.

"That's enough, Duke," he ordered. "I'll handle this in my own way."

Then he turned back to the rest of the team.

"I don't know how those cigarettes got into Danny Orlis's pocket, guys, but I do know this much. If he says that they aren't his, and that he hasn't been smoking, and Larry backs him up in it, that's good enough for me."

"How come?" Duke persisted, his lips curling sarcastically.

"Because I've never known Danny to tell a lie since he first came here," the coach replied evenly. "And since Larry was released from the detention center, he's never lied to me that I know of, or to any of the other teachers. When a guy gets a reputation for telling the truth, you believe him when he tells you something."

Danny started to get into his second-team uniform when Coach Edwards stopped him.

"Here," the basketball mentor said, "you'd better put on this first-team uniform. I'm going to see what you can do against Norwood tonight."

For an instant Danny could scarcely believe what he had heard.

"Do you mean that I'm going to get to play with the first team tonight?" he asked excitedly. His heart rose to his throat and began to hammer there.

"Yes," Coach Edwards answered. "I'm going to give both you and Duke a chance. We need one of you on the first string." With that he turned abruptly and stalked out of the dressing room.

"Wow," Danny said almost to himself, "I'm going to get a chance to play with the first string. And against Norwood too! Just think of that!"

"You lucky guy," Larry replied enviously.

"I break out in a sweat just thinking about it," Danny went on. "I don't know what I'll be able to do out there before all those people."

"If you don't want to try," Larry said, laughing, "just let me know, and I'll go in your place."

Danny looked at his cousin quickly. In spite of the smile on Larry's face there had been something peculiar in his tone, a touch of sarcasm or jealousy.

The second-team game seemed to drag on for-ever. Without Danny and Duke, the Iron Mountain team was badly handicapped in the goal-making department. When the game finally drew to a close, Norwood had won by a sizable margin.

"All right, guys," Coach Edwards said to the first team. "Let's get out there now and show them how to play basketball."

Cold, nervous sweat stood out on Danny's forehead and the palms of his hands as they warmed up. He was thankful for one thing—he wasn't going to start.

DANNY IS OUTCLASSED

Norwood had as good a first team as the papers had said they had. And during the first quarter they jumped into a commanding lead. Coach Edwards alternated Duke at forward with the starter in that position. Danny sat on the sidelines until midway in the second quarter.

"All right, Orlis," Coach Edwards said during a brief lull in the furious action, "go in for Duke."

Danny felt his nerves tighten like the strings on a violin, and his hands trembled as he reported to the referee. This was it. If he didn't make good this time, he might never get another chance!

"They'll slaughter you, Orlis," Duke snarled under his breath as he passed him.

Play resumed just then, and Norwood took the ball and started slowly down the court. Danny's man dribbled toward him carefully and deliberately. Then, when he was only a pace or so away, he faked to the left, and with a sudden burst of speed slipped past Danny and dribbled in under the basket for an easy goal.

"Watch him, Danny!" the Iron Mountain captain called from across the court. "Watch that guy! He's tricky!"

With that goal the game exploded into action so furious that Danny was left bewildered and floundering. It was one thing to dribble and handle the ball when moving at a comfortable pace, and quite another to do the same thing racing headlong down the court.

They faked him out of position, stole the ball from him, and caused him to foul three times in as many minutes in a desperate effort to keep up with the game. In a scant five minutes Coach Edwards sent Duke back in and jerked Danny.

"What did I tell you, Danny?" Duke chortled as he trotted onto the floor. "What did I tell you?"

Coach Edwards motioned Danny to sit down beside him.

"I'm sorry, Danny," he said softly. "I really thought that you could make it. But I guess it's too much to expect a fellow to master all the fundamentals of a game like this in a few short weeks—especially when he's never played before. Maybe next year."

Danny felt the lump grow in his throat. It was hard to see Duke out there mastering the position that he had failed in. And yet he couldn't blame Duke or

Coach Edwards or anyone else except himself. He just didn't know enough about basketball. That was all.

"That was a tough break, Danny," Bob said as they walked home after the game. "Maybe you'll get another chance."

Danny shook his head. "Not this year," he said. "Coach Edwards as good as told me that this evening. I'm going to stay out with the second team, though, for as long as he'll let me."

In the days that followed, Mr. Hanson, the biology teacher, continued to point out the places where the story of rocks and fossils and evolution differed from the Bible's account of Creation. However, he remained true to his word not to hold Danny or anyone else up to ridicule. He even dealt sternly with anyone in the class who tried to do so.

Bob was so hungry to hear the teacher that more than once he skipped basketball practice and stayed after school to ask questions or get some books the instructor had suggested he read.

"I'd like to believe the way you and Larry do, Danny," Bob said one night as they sat in the basement eating popcorn and talking. "But you've got to admit that what Mr. Hanson says does make sense. There is absolute proof that the world is millions and millions of years old and that all life evolved from simpler forms of life."

Danny reached for another handful of popcorn but said nothing.

"It fits into the things we were taught in the fourth, fifth, and sixth grades," he went on, "about the three-toed animal that evolved into the horse and things like that. I–I'd like to believe what the Bible says, but when you see such proof as that, you just can't. You can't argue with science."

Danny sat there for a long time. He should say something. He had to speak up, but he didn't know how to answer Bob.

"I don't care," he said at last, "what sort of proof they've got which they claim disproves the Bible. I'll stack the Bible up against a science book any day."

Bob was unimpressed.

"You've got to prove it to me," he said.

Danny's heart ached as he listened to his cousin's doubts. With him it didn't make too much difference what Mr. Hanson or anyone else said about the Bible—he still believed that it was the Word of God and that every word was true. But Bob was such a new Christian that it was easy for him to get all mixed up. It was a matter he and Larry were praying about.

The next afternoon the two boys sought the help of Pastor Johnson.

"This is something serious, boys," he said when they told him the story. "And I'm so glad that you came to me."

"We thought maybe you had some proof or something that would help us explain the truth to Bob," Danny said, "something that would make him see that all science doesn't attack the Bible."

"Yes," Pastor Johnson replied, walking over to the bookshelves in his study, "I've got good authoritative books that will prove to you, or any other fair-minded person, that true science and the Bible go hand in hand."

He stopped a moment.

"I'm not sure, though, that it's best to use them in a classroom to try to embarrass your teacher. I really doubt whether any lasting good can come from that sort of thing."

"But isn't there something that we can do?" Danny asked seriously. "Bob's just a new Christian and he's getting all mixed up. Isn't there some way we can help him to get straightened out?"

The pastor was silent for a long while. "There must be something that we can do," he said. "I'll tell you what, boys. Let's make it a real matter of prayer. Then you get in touch with me in a few days."

CHAPTER 10

THE INDIANS NEED THE GOSPEL

The next few days Danny and Larry were so busy that they didn't have time to get in touch with Pastor Johnson as he had asked them to do. They each had a book review to write for English before Friday afternoon and, with two tough second-team games coming up over the weekend, Coach Edwards enlisted the aid of one of the other teachers to help with the coaching and sent the second squad into extra-long practice sessions.

"What are you doing here with the second team, Danny?" Duke asked sarcastically as they met in the locker room. "I thought you boasted that you were going to be on the first string or you weren't going to play basketball at all."

"Not me," Danny grinned. "I think I'm lucky to be playing on the second team."

"You can say that again," Duke snapped. He swaggered halfway across the dressing room, then turned and called to Danny. "You'd better stick to your preaching and let me do the basketball playing from here on out," he retorted.

Two or three of the guys snickered at Danny derisively.

"I'm afraid I'm not much good at either one," he said, and calmly went on tying his shoelaces.

"That Duke," Larry said as he and Danny walked home in the semidarkness. "Just because he's got a brother who's a prize fighter and he can lick most of the guys at school, he thinks he can run over us any time he feels like it."

"I'm not afraid of him," Danny said simply. "Up where I live a guy's got to know how to take care of himself. But I just don't see any point in getting all excited and worked up about a guy like him. I'm a lot more worried about Bob and this science business."

At that very moment Bob came up behind them.

"Now what are you worried about me for?" he laughingly asked.

"You ought to know," Danny told him.

They walked along in silence for half a block or so.

"Say, Danny," Bob said suddenly, "have your parents written anything about that Indian family we met during Christmas vacation? The Bedeans?"

"Mom says something about them every once in a while," Danny answered. "Why?"

"For some reason I've been thinking about them quite a lot the last few days," he replied. "Did she ever say whether Big John had become a Christian or not?"

"I don't think that he has, Bob," Danny answered. "With the post office and everything, my parents aren't able to get out much. And there isn't anyone else to go and talk with them about Christ."

"That's the thing that gets me," Bob said seriously. "There's that Indian family, just waiting for someone to talk to them about Jesus, but there's no one to do it." He paused for a while. "You know," he went on at last, "if something happened and they died before they accepted Christ as their Savior I–I'd feel as though it would be my fault–that I'd be to blame."

The boys walked on across the street and over a block to their home.

"You know," Danny said softly at last, "it might be that the Lord is trying to tell you that He wants you to serve Him."

"What do you mean?" Bob asked.

"He might be telling you that you should prepare yourself to go among people like that with the Gospel."

"I don't see what that's got to do with it," he said thoughtfully.

"God might want you as a missionary," Danny continued. "He uses a lot of different ways to get us to do His will. He might be talking to you that way, telling you that He wants you to serve Him up in our area among the Indians."

A faraway look came into Bob's eyes.

"Do you suppose that God might want to use me that way?" he asked, more of himself than of his companions.

Larry looked over at Danny and smiled happily. It made him feel good just to hear Bob talk that way.

But it was different the next afternoon in biology. Mr. Hanson again took up the subject of the origin of man.

Looking directly at Danny, he said, "I know that this subject is one that causes a great deal of argument and difference of opinion. I'm not bringing it up to argue or to hurt the faith of anyone. Yet this is something that must be faced."

Danny Orlis squirmed uncomfortably in his seat and cast a quick glance at Bob. He was leaning forward, his pencil poised above his notebook, ready to take down every word the instructor said.

"It is a surprising thing," Mr. Hanson went on, "that of all the archaeological crews that have been out and the findings that have been made, that the true intermediary creature between man and other mammals on the evolutionary ladder has not been discovered. However, there is ample evidence to prove–"

Mr. Hanson droned on and on. Danny tried to stay interested, but he had read all that the teacher was saying in biology books. And, in spite of himself, his mind wandered back to the Northwest Angle, his dog, Laddie, and his parents.

He looked over at Bob again. His older cousin was taking notes furiously.

When the class was over, Larry came up to where Danny was standing.

"Did you notice Bob?" he asked. "He acted as though he had never heard anything so wonderful."

Danny nodded and picked up his books.

CHAPTER 11

FINDING THE BETTER WAY

The next day's lesson in biology was a continuation of the day before, and Mr. Hanson assigned a list of reference books to be read over the weekend.

"This is Thursday," he said, "and I'm going to have you write a theme on the origin of man. You are to have it ready by Monday afternoon."

Bob had been listening and asking questions and reading stacks of biology books, but Danny and Larry hadn't realized just how it was affecting him until that evening when they got ready to go to youth group.

"Are you about ready, Bob?" Danny called to him from the living room.

His older cousin came to the door of his room with a thick book in his hand.

"I don't think I'm going tonight," he said carelessly. "I've got other things to do."

"But there is youth group tonight," Larry protested. "You don't want to miss that!"

"I know," Bob said indifferently. "But I want to read some of these books that Mr. Hanson lent me. They really go into this evolution business in a way that anybody can understand."

When the boys saw Pastor Johnson that evening after youth group and told him what had happened, he got to his feet and reached for his hat.

"I'll take you boys home," he said. "I've been giving this matter a good deal of thought and prayer. I want to talk to your parents, Larry. This is something that the church and the home must tackle together."

Danny leaned back in the seat of Pastor Johnson's car. He felt better already. The minister went at things about the way that his dad did, thinking and praying them through carefully, and then acting. It was good to have someone like that helping them.

"I had never dreamed they were teaching anything like that in school," Danny's Uncle Claude said when Pastor Johnson had related the story to him. "How long has this been going on, anyway?"

"We got some of it in the fourth and fifth grades," Larry put in. "Of course, we didn't know what it was then."

Uncle Claude got to his feet.

"I'm going right over to that school superintendent," he said. "I'll put a stop to that sort of thing right now."

"Don't do that, Dad," Larry cut in quickly. "Don't, please! We'll be the laughingstock of the school if you do!"

"But I can't let them ruin Bob's faith," he said.

"It won't do any good to go and talk to them," Larry went on desperately. "That would just make things worse."

"But I've got to do something!" his dad countered.

"I'm rather inclined to agree with Larry," Pastor Johnson said. "I think I have a plan that will help."

Uncle Claude crossed the room nervously and sat down.

"If we can organize a high school Bible Club," the minister went on, "we can help to band the Christian kids together and give them the Christian answer to things like this evolution teaching in biology, high school issues, and a good many other things."

As he explained how the Bible Club would be organized and what it would accomplish, Danny found himself getting excited.

"I'll say we'll help," he told Pastor Johnson. "Larry and I will do everything we can to get it going."

The two boys were so excited that night that they could scarcely get to sleep. But the next morning they didn't dare say anything about it on the way to school. Pastor Johnson had asked them to keep it quiet until the plans had been a little better laid.

"I'll see you second period, Larry," Danny said as they stopped for a moment at the door of the schoolhouse.

Just then someone grabbed Danny by the arm and spun him around.

"Hey!" he cried in surprise. "What's the big idea?"

Then he saw that it was Duke. His face was drawn and livid with rage.

"You know what the big idea is!" Duke gritted. "You were jealous because I got on the first team and you didn't, so you tattled on me!"

"Tattled on you?" Danny echoed. "What do you mean?"

"You know what I mean!" Duke retorted. "You snitched to Coach Edwards about my smoking and got me kicked off the team! Now I'm going to beat you to a pulp!"

CHAPTER 12

ONE GIRL'S INFLUENCE

"I'll fix you, Danny Orlis!" Duke snarled, advancing toward him with his fists clenched menacingly.

"Just a minute," Danny said, taking a step backward, "I don't want to fight with you or anyone else."

"You're a coward!" Duke whispered tensely. "That's what you are! A coward!"

Danny looked at him and grinned. "What makes you think that I'm afraid of you, Duke?" he asked evenly.

"I'll show you!" By this time Duke's face was white with rage, and his hands were trembling. "I'll show you why you ought to be afraid of me!"

Just then the school principal came up.

"What's going on?" he asked brusquely, looking straight at Duke.

Duke dropped his arms to his sides and took a step or two backward. The color rose in his cheeks. "N-n-nothing," he stammered. "Nothing at all."

"Don't tell me that, Duke," the principal retorted. "I've been watching you." He paused for a moment. "You had better come to my office, young man. I want to talk to you."

As Duke passed Danny he whispered threateningly, "Just you wait until I get you out somewhere alone!"

"Duke," Mr. Brown called to him, "I'm waiting." Danny watched until the two disappeared into the principal's office. It was an hour or more before Duke, his cheeks pale and drawn, returned to class.

* * * *

That afternoon when the guys reported to the gym for basketball practice Coach Edwards was grim.

"Most of you already know that Duke has been kicked off the team for smoking," he said. "That's going to put a strain on all the rest of you. We've been counting on him for the tough games that we've got coming up. But, if you all do your part, we'll get along."

He started the practice session with the first squad, but as soon as he got them to scrimmaging, he came over and watched the second team. After a few minutes he sounded his whistle and called Danny over to him.

"You're looking better out there, Orlis," he said. "How's the ball handling?"

"I'm doing the best I can."

"Are you getting a little confidence in yourself," he persisted, "so you can go out on the floor and play without thinking about missing a pass or getting your feet tangled up while you're dribbling?"

"I think so," Danny replied.

"Well," Coach Edwards said shortly, "we'll try you with the first team again tomorrow night."

For a moment or two Danny stood there before moving out to his position. Now Duke surely would think that he had been the one who had squealed on him for smoking.

* * * *

Pastor Johnson hadn't wasted any time in getting the information about organizing the Bible Club and setting up the first meeting. In little more than a week he came to see Danny and Larry to outline the final plans.

"Peggy Denton volunteered to have the first meeting in her home," he said. "And she's going to talk with her friends and acquaintances about coming. I'm going to count on you two to get some of the younger guys and girls."

"I don't know, Danny," Bob said indifferently when they asked him. "I'm going to be pretty busy for anything like that."

"But this won't take a lot of time," Danny persisted. "And, besides, it will give you a good chance to study the Bible."

Bob crossed over to his desk and sat down. "To tell you the truth," he said, "it might just be a waste of time to study a Book as unscientific and full of errors as the Bible is."

Danny sat there miserably, searching for words.

"But I–I thought you were planning on the mission field," he protested. "I thought you were going to go up to the Angle and take the Gospel to those Indians who have never heard it!"

Bob's face grew serious. Slowly he picked up the Bible and held it tenderly. "If I just knew whether this Book is true!" he whispered. "I'd go in a minute, if I knew!"

Danny sat there helplessly, a prayer for his cousin in his heart.

"There are some things that we just have to trust God in," he said lamely. That explanation satisfied him, but even as he spoke, he knew that it didn't help Bob at all.

Larry and Danny and Peggy met several times to work out the details of the first meeting.

"This is the most important meeting that we'll have," Peggy said excitedly. "Everything's got to be right."

The boys nodded their agreement.

"Is Bob going to talk to his friends about coming?" she asked.

The smile left Larry's face.

"We don't even think he's coming," he said.

"Oh, but he's got to," she replied determinedly. "He's just got to."

"We can't do anything with him," Danny said. "Why don't you ask him?"

"I–I couldn't do that," Peggy stammered, her cheeks coloring. And then she stopped. "Do–do you think he'd come if I did?" she asked.

"He might."

Danny and Larry didn't have a chance to talk to Bob the next morning, but the following evening after supper, when they were getting ready to go to the first Bible Club meeting, he came down to their room in the basement.

"Can I borrow a clean pair of socks, Larry?" he asked.

"Sure," his brother replied. "Help yourself."

"I figured that I might go to the Bible Club meeting tonight with you guys," he continued.

"Great."

Bob sat down on the side of the bed and began to pull on the socks he had borrowed.

"You know," he said after a time, "that Peggy Denton is a great girl."

Larry and Danny both nodded. "She's a wonderful Christian girl."

"She hunted me out and asked me to go tonight," Bob went on. "She must have talked with half the guys and girls in school. She was so nice and so friendly that I just couldn't say no."

There was a good turnout for the first meeting of the Bible Club, and everybody seemed to have a good time.

"This is going to be a lot of fun," Bob said enthusiastically on the way home. "I wouldn't miss it for anything!"

CHAPTER 13

THE SQUAD IS REINFORCED

Duke had heard that Danny was practicing with the first squad, but he didn't say anything. In fact, he usually looked the other way when Danny met him in the hall. The other guys all talked about how hard Duke was taking his dismissal from the team.

"It was really rough on him," one of them said. "He hasn't smoked or even gone out anywhere nights since Coach Edwards kicked him off the team."

Danny felt a sharp stab of pain when he heard them. He knew just how Duke must feel.

Nevertheless, he did the best he could to hold his position on the first squad. But he still had trouble handling the ball when the pace got hot, and every now and then he traveled or got his feet tangled when he tried to dribble. The coach worked with him patiently.

"Just don't get excited, Danny," he said. "Keep your head and take those passes as they come. You can handle them."

He nodded uncertainly. He was never sure of anything in basketball.

For some reason, Danny didn't quite know why, Duke kept preying on his mind. He had wanted so badly to play against Creston. And the team needed him too. For a long time the night before the game Danny prayed about it. The next morning he went to Coach Edwards' office.

"I–I was just wondering, Coach," he began uncertainly, "Do you think that Duke has learned his lesson about smoking?"

"What do you mean?" the coach asked.

"The guys all say that Duke hasn't smoked or even gone anywhere nights since that time you caught him," Danny went on. "I thought perhaps you ought to know it. I–I figured maybe you'd give him another chance."

Coach Edwards picked up a pencil and held it in both hands momentarily. "I'm glad to hear about Duke," he said. "We certainly need him."

He paused for some time.

"But you know what that means, don't you, if I do take him back?"

Danny nodded. "I–I'm afraid I can't play well enough to be on the first team anyway."

The coach didn't say whether he intended to give Duke a second chance or not. He stood there a moment or two, staring past Danny, then mumbled something and walked off.

However, the next afternoon Duke was out for practice with the rest of the team. He came into the dressing room late and went directly to his locker without looking at anyone.

"Hi, Duke," one of the guys said when he saw him.

"Hi," he grunted.

Danny wanted to go over and speak to him, but when their eyes met Duke flushed and turned quickly away.

"Hurry up, you guys," an assistant called loudly, sticking his head in the doorway.

Danny tossed his shoes into the bottom of his locker and started out. "Come on, Larry, let's go."

"Hey," Larry said as they trotted out onto the gym floor, "I was surprised to see Duke back today. I thought the coach kicked him off for good."

"He did," Duke answered shortly from behind them.

Larry whirled, startled.

"He did kick me off the team," Duke repeated, "but Danny, here, got scared that I'd knock his teeth in and begged Coach Edwards to take me back."

He laughed ironically and went running over to where the first team had gathered.

"Did you go to Coach Edwards?" Larry asked.

Danny nodded.

"But why?" Larry wanted to know. "You would have been on the first team yourself if Duke hadn't gotten back. And after all he's done to you!"

Danny grinned and took his place at forward with the rest of the second squad.

After practice Danny was a little slow in getting dressed, and the rest of the guys had gone on and left him. It was almost dark when he came out of the schoolhouse and cut across the lawn.

"Hello, Danny," somebody said behind him.

He turned quickly. It was Duke Millington, standing with his hands in his pockets beside an evergreen tree.

"Hello, Duke," he said, stopping. "I didn't see you there."

For two full minutes the other boy didn't say a word. His eyes were fixed on something far beyond.

"I–I want to talk to you, Danny," he said at last.

CHAPTER 14

DUKE AND DANNY SETTLE THE SCORE

"**S**ure thing," Danny said.

"I–I don't know just how to begin, Danny," Duke stammered, shifting nervously from one foot to the other. "I've been a jerk."

Danny smiled warmly. Duke gulped hard.

"Coach Edwards called me in yesterday," the older basketball player went on, "and told me that you had talked him into giving me another chance with the team."

Danny said nothing. Somehow it embarrassed him to have Duke standing there biting at his lower lip and forcing out the words.

"I'm sorry that I've treated you so mean," Duke Millington went on. "I've done everything that I could to keep you off the first team. I've made fun of you to the other guys and everything else. Even today, after I knew what you had done for me, I–I had to ridicule you in front of the rest of the guys."

"That's all right," Danny said quietly. "That sort of stuff doesn't bother me."

"I know," Duke blurted, "but it bothers me. I want you to know that I'm sorry for all the things that I've said and done."

"That's okay," Danny replied, holding out his hand impulsively, "this is better than fighting, isn't it?"

"You–you're a great guy, Danny," Duke said, his voice choking.

"You're okay, too, Duke," answered Danny. "I also know that you're a lot better on the basketball court than I am."

The two of them fell in step as they walked down the street together. Danny smiled broadly. It was good to be friends with Duke.

"I'm through smoking and breaking training," Duke said after a time. "I sure learned my lesson on that deal. And I know now that you didn't tattle on me, either. A guy can't get by with that stuff very long. Somebody's sure to find out."

"That's right," Danny answered. "And I'm glad that you aren't going to break training anymore." He paused a moment or two. "But there's something a lot more important than that. If we really want our lives changed, we must confess that we are sinners and put our whole trust in Christ. When we've done that, then we're changed."

"I never did go much for religion," Duke retorted, bristling a little.

"I'm not talking about religion," Danny replied. "I'm talking about being a Christian. That isn't only religion, it's a whole way of life."

"It all sounds good," Duke acknowledged, "but how can you know what to believe when the Bible's so full of myths and mistakes and contradictions?"

"Like what?" Danny asked him.

For a moment Duke was silent. Then he said, "Oh, there are lots of them. All you have to do is study zoology and biology a little. Take all that stuff about the world being created in six days for example. Nobody believes that anymore."

"I know what some biology and zoology books say," Danny answered, "and I know and believe what the Word of God says."

"But how can you get around the proof that scientists have?" Duke asked seriously. "How do you explain them away?"

"I don't have all the answers," said Danny, "but if you'll come to Bible Club with me, you'll get the answers there. Pastor Johnson is going to introduce our new sponsor, and the first subject we're going to take up is evolution and the Bible."

"I don't know," Duke said, hesitating, "I never did have much to do with the church."

"This isn't like church," Danny countered. "We just meet around in the different kids' homes and sing and study the Bible and have good times together."

"They'd probably fall over in a faint if they saw me come in," Duke protested.

"A lot of the guys are coming to Bible Club. Larry and I will stop by for you. How about it?"

The Bible Club met at Larry and Bob's place the next evening, but Danny got ready early and went after Duke.

"I've decided not to go," Duke said. "I've got a lot of studying to do."

"We'll be out early," Danny told him.

When the two of them came into the living room where the Bible Club was meeting, everyone turned and stared at them. The color came up in Duke's face, and he hesitated a moment until Larry and Pastor Johnson came over to speak to him.

After the meeting opened, and they had sung a few choruses, Pastor Johnson said, "I'm very happy to present to you a local Christian businessman who has studied archaeology extensively. I know we'll all enjoy and profit from his helpful instruction. Mr. Don Saunders."

Danny looked over at Bob who was eying the speaker carefully. Mr. Saunders got up and started to talk to them. It wasn't like a sermon at all or one of the lectures at school. Instead, he just talked. He explained how the Bible didn't contradict true science and that many outstanding Bible scholars had other explanations for the apparent age of rocks and oil and coal.

"Of course," he said, "we don't hold with the theory—and it is only a theory—that man was produced by evolution, or that any species of animal evolved out of another."

Bob's hand went up instantly. "I read just a few weeks ago about a scientist who was flying down to South Africa where they had caught some sort of fish that he claimed was the link between fish and reptiles," he said. "What about that?"

Mr. Saunders smiled.

"We'll have to have that proved to us," he said. "It reminds me of the so-called 'monkey trial' that William Jennings Bryan figured in years ago. One of the witnesses testified that a 'Nebraska Man' had been discovered that proved man had been on this earth millions and millions of years and had also developed tremendously during that time. They learned all of this, they said, from the fragment of his skull which they had unearthed. But, you know, a couple of years later somebody discovered the rest of that 'man'—only it turned out that he wasn't a man at all, but a prehistoric pig."

The kids snickered appreciatively, and Danny glanced quickly at Duke. Mr. Saunders was making a real impression.

"So," the sponsor concluded. "You can't always tell what is true and what isn't by what some so-called scientist happens to guess."

The room was quiet for a couple of minutes, then Bob turned to Peggy and whispered loud enough so that Danny could hear. "Just the same, there must be something to this evolution business or all the smart scientists wouldn't believe it."

Peggy looked appealingly at Danny.

CHAPTER 15

ROCKS AND CLIFF UNDER INSPECTION

The next morning Peggy was waiting for Danny in the corridor at school.

"I'm so worried about Bob," she said. "He believes everything that Mr. Hanson tells him and everything he reads in those science books that he's always taking home."

"I know," Danny answered.

"Just last night," she went on, "he said that the Bible and science couldn't both be right and that he had about decided to quit going to church or Bible Club, that the whole business was just a bunch of fancy stories—I'm awfully worried about him, Danny!"

Danny nodded in agreement. "I know," he said.

At the next Bible Club meeting, however, Bob again led the discussion around to evolution, and the scientific errors in the Bible.

"The whole history is in the rocks, Mr. Saunders," he said, "and it proves absolutely that evolution is true, and that the Bible story is false."

Mr. Saunders was silent a moment. "Just what makes you think that?" he asked quietly.

"Science proves it," Bob repeated. "The oldest fossils of invertebrates are found in the oldest rocks, and the fishes are found in younger rocks. Animals are in still younger rocks. The proof is right there where no one can deny it."

Danny leaned forward expectantly, waiting for the answer.

"Have you ever seen fossils in rocks, Bob?" Mr. Saunders asked.

"I've seen plenty of pictures," the younger boy retorted.

"How would you like to go back into the hills Saturday and see them for yourself?" the sponsor asked. "I'd like to wait to answer your question until I can show you what I mean."

"Sure thing," Bob and half a dozen others echoed.

"Good enough," Mr. Saunders said. "Anybody who wants to go can meet at my house at nine o'clock Saturday morning."

Danny had hoped that the whole club would be able to make the trip, but when nine o'clock came only half a dozen boys and two girls besides Peggy had come.

The club sponsor drove some fifteen or twenty miles on the paved highway back into the mountains, then turned at the foot of a mountain and drove up a narrow, twisting, gravel road for two or three miles farther.

"Everybody out!" Mr. Saunders ordered, grinding to a stop.

"Is this where the fossils are?" Bob asked.

"Oh, no," Don Saunders said, "you're going to have to work a little before you get a look at them."

"How did you ever happen to find a place like this anyway?" Duke asked as they started to trudge up the mountain trail.

"I was on an archaeology team when I was going to school at Harvard," Don said. "We spent a summer poking around up here. We found them then."

"You were on a Harvard archaeology team?" Bob echoed.

"I would have graduated if the war hadn't come along," Mr. Saunders answered him. "As a matter of fact, I majored in archaeology."

"You did?" Bob repeated, as though he couldn't bring himself to believe it. "And you still believe that science is wrong and the Bible is true?"

"Let's put it this way, Bob," Don Saunders said. "I believe that if a theory differs with the Bible, then it's not science."

Bob looked at the Bible Club leader with new respect, and then at Duke Millington who was standing open-mouthed at his side.

A few minutes later Don Saunders stopped the group at the base of a cliff that seemed to tower above them for thousands and thousands of feet.

"This is what you've been talking about, isn't it, Bob?" he asked.

"That's right," Bob said excitedly. "And right there are the fossils!"

For several minutes the group examined the fossils along the cliff.

"This proves that science is right," Bob exclaimed enthusiastically.

"But these fossils are of mammals," Mr. Saunders countered, "and belong to the Tertiary Geological Age. In other words, they're comparatively young in age as fossils are counted. Yet they are in the bottom layer. The next layer contains fossils of fish, the next is of reptiles, and the amphibians and invertebrates are on top. According to the way some scientists tell the story of the rocks, everything on this mountain is upside down. The species that are supposed to be the oldest are the youngest here. And those that are called the youngest are the oldest. How do you account for that?"

"This is what is referred to as a 'thrust fault,' isn't it?" Bob asked.

"That's what they call it," Don Saunders went on. "They say that somehow or in some way these earlier layers got thrust up and the others were thrust underneath. But just look up at the cliff. The rock formation is the same. There isn't any line to show that one layer was formed at a different time than the layer above or below it. Those layers are hundreds of feet thick and at least a mile or two long. Does the theory of a 'rock thrust' sound believable to you?"

Nobody said a word.

"But what does this have to do with the Bible and evolution?" Duke Millington asked. His voice was strained and choked.

"This is the very heart of the archaeologist's proof of evolution," Mr. Saunders went on. "His theory goes something like this: the fossils of the simplest forms of life are the oldest. Those of the more complex creatures are progressively younger, just like the rungs in a ladder, until they get to the age of man. Therefore, he says, all life evolved from the simplest form of life. The Bible account says that God created all life. Which are we to believe?"

Bob's face was drawn. He stared at the rocks and then back at Mr. Saunders.

"I–I–" he began uncertainly.

Duke Millington, who had been standing next to Danny, turned to him.

"I've been a fool, Danny," he said in a hoarse whisper.

"You can fix that up right now, Duke," Danny answered.

"But would God want a guy like me?"

"He wants everyone who will put his trust in Him," Danny replied. "Why don't you take care of that now?"

Together Danny and Duke knelt off to one side of the little group. Mr. Saunders saw what was happening and led the others away.

Bob went over to where the sponsor was standing.

"I want to thank you," he said. "You helped me get the right slant on a lot of things. I know now that the Bible is the Word of God, and that it's true—every word of it."

"I'm glad of that, Bob. We've all been praying for you. Some of these things we have to take on faith, but wherever there is any real evidence, it supports the Word of God."

Bob nodded seriously. Then his gaze met Peggy's. She smiled happily, her eyes glistening with tears.

THE DANNY ORLIS SERIES

The Danny Orlis series, by Bernard Palmer, delivers a blend of adventure, mystery, and suspense through various settings—from the Canadian wilderness to Guatemalan jungles. Danny Orlis, an adept outdoorsman, skilled athlete, and committed Christian, employs his quick thinking, calm bravery, and biblical solutions to confront everyday problems and hair-raising dangers. Early stories focus on Danny navigating school life, sports, and outdoor challenges, while in later books, Danny and his wife Kay provide wisdom and guidance to youngsters facing lifelike situations and challenges. Having sold over two million copies, this series has made Palmer a renowned author in Christian youth literature. Palmer is also the author of the Felicia Cartright series and various other series for Christian youth.

AVAILABLE FROM WWW.ANEKOPRESS.COM

www.ingramcontent.com/pod-product-compliance
Lightning Source LLC
Chambersburg PA
CBHW071535120726
47907CB00014B/2265